Carl The Chameleon

(Book Two of the Kids' Compass Series)

Carl The Chameleon

Written and Illustrated
by
Todd Schimmell

Art Director
Kirsten Schimmell

a Compassio Veraque LLC imprint

ISBN: 978-1-7352463-6-9

printed in the United States of America

Carl was a quirky chameleon,
Who changed colors by the gazillion.

No matter what time, or even the mood,
His bright colors would match his attitude.

When he was red,

he warned, "Stay away!"

Orange meant
Carl wanted to
PLAY!

He was always silly
when he wore pink.

Blue said he was having
deep thoughts to think.

Yellow brought with it,
"Carl The Brave!"

Purple announced
he wouldn't behave.

One day Carl found glasses near his tree.

He put them on and they fit perfectly.

He looked down and noticed he was bright green? He felt bold so brown should have been seen.

His color stayed green it did not change.

This was downright weird, confusing, and strange.

He felt upset so he should have been gray.

Nope, still green-did his colors fly away?

He was known for his color changing skin. Who was he if not? "Oh, where to begin?

A green chameleon? Gasp! What a bore!

Is there more to me? I'll need to explore."

He asked Tree Frog, "What do you think of me?"

"You're a great climber that's easy to see."

"My dear Iguana what am I to you?"
"Why, you're a best friend tried and true!"

"Toucan, looking at me what comes to mind?"

"I'd say you're funny and one of a kind!"

Maybe my skin doesn't set me apart? It's a part of me but just the start. He removed his glasses and colors showed through. He was deep thinking, and his skin was blue.

It was those glasses making him see green, but to his friends his colors went unseen.

They noticed the things that were not skin deep.

Carl grinned as his heart skipped a beat!

The green glasses helped Carl to see,
what his friends already knew him to be.

He turned green so he was feeling okay.
It's not who he was, just his color today.

KIDS' COMPASS QUESTIONS

1. Do we notice how other people look?

2. Does that change how we feel about them?

3. Are you more than just how you look?

4. What are some things besides how you look, that make you great?

If you're reading with a friend, tell them the things you like about them.

Todd Schimmell's Other Titles

(Available online wherever books are sold)

Children's Books

The Elephant Tooted

The Fun Reader (Adults Beware)

The Book That Stunk (Adults Beware)

All Ages Illustrated Poetry Books

Pass The Time

Smile and Soul

Teen to Adult Poetry Books

Nursery Rhymes for Humanity

Nursery Rhymes for Humanity Volume II

About The Author

Todd Schimmell is a happily married father of four and a school resource officer in Indiana. He welcomes reader comments on

Facebook: @authortoddschimmell

Instagram: @authortodd

and invites you to join him at authortodd.com

Made in the USA
Columbia, SC
17 February 2022

56379007R00020